RUBY

Ernie Howard

Ernie Howard
Visit my website at
www.erniehowardwrites.com

Printed in the United States of America

First Printing: Sep 2020
One Eight Infinite
ISBN: 9798690837389

DEDICATION

To my wife and three boys.

CONTENTS

ACKNOWLEDGMENTS

"SHAKESPEARE WROTE MOBY-
DICK, USING MELVILLE AS A OUIJA
BOARD."
— **RAY BRADBURY**

1 RUBY

A NIGHT PORTALS SHORT STORY

He could feel his fingers becoming part of the game piece. They were dissolving into the plastic of the planchette as the thing made its way around the board. He wasn't paying any attention to what letters it was choosing to spell out his doom. He had stopped screaming a few minutes ago, and now he sat frozen in horror. The more he tried to pull his hand away, the more his fingers and now his hand sunk deeper into the game piece, going somewhere else. It was an off feeling. The air in the room was stuffy, but the devoured parts of his fingertips were cool. Like he had them in a cup of ice water.

"Pleeeease." His voice came out in a wheezing whine. The thing that stood in front of him didn't reply. It just kept reciting the letters that the planchette fell on.

"D-O-O-M-E-D-T-I-M-E-T-O-P-A-Y."

"No, please. I'm sorry." Scott said. The game piece gobbled up his hand and stopped mid-forearm.

"T-I-M-E-T-O-F-E-E-L-M-Y-P-A-I-N."

Scott realized then that the thing standing in front of him had only been playing with him. The planchette stop in the middle of the board. The thing snapped its gnarled fingers, and he screamed once more as the game piece opened up, and his whole body flew through into a gaping cold hole. It consumed all of the man, much like a snake would swallow a mouse.

The house went immediately silent. The thing standing before the table watched as the planchette moved around and spelled out a message.

"I-T-I-S-D-O-N-E-2-M-O-R-E"

The thing smiled a crooked smile and started to change back to something less grotesque.

****

Ruby Worklow was a tall woman with large features. She wasn't hard to look at or what people would call ugly. People liked to look at Ruby. She was just immense. Her full blond hair sat on a large head that sat on a thick neck connected to broad shoulders. She was big right down to her size thirteen feet. That's why people would sit with their mouths opened wide when they first heard her voice. People always expected low bass. Instead, her voice came out in a soft, confident tone that set people at ease and immediately made them like her. It was Ruby's unique form of hypnosis. How could such a sweet, comforting voice come out of this giant of a woman; they would say. At least that is what most people would say if you were one of the people who liked Ruby.

Victor wasn't buying it anymore.

"She's creepy, Sara," Victor said. He was mindlessly clicking through cooking shows and reality TV. The screens changed with each press of the button, making the dark living room light up into different shade of blues and reds.

Sara rolled her eyes as she scrawled through her Facebook feed and thought for the hundredth time why she didn't just delete this time-consuming train wreck. "Victor, why all of a sudden do you think she's creepy? Weren't you sort of friends with her in high school? Better friends than I was. I barely knew you let alone, Ruby."

"That's because you were one of the cool kids." Sara hit his arm without looking up from her phone. Sometimes Victor hated the fact that he and his wife had gone to school together. It meant that he couldn't get away with any half-truths when it came to old acquaintances. Sara didn't know everything, though.

"Hey, you don't have to convince me. She always seemed kind of weird. Remember when she would mumble that strange made-up language in class?" Victor nodded his head and tried to conceal the shiver that went up to his back. "I thought it was weird that she reached out to me at Scott's funeral. I don't think we spoke two words to each other when we were kids. She seems pretty normal now, though."

She was normal, Victor thought. At least up until… His mind went blank. Some memory was going to pop up and then like air blew away. Victor looked at his wife all of a sudden, scared that she could read his thoughts. What would she be reading,

Victor? You can't remember anything yourself, he thought. "I've talked to a lot of people, Sara. She was there with Mary, Chuck, and Scott. She's always there." Victor said.

"What do you mean, there?" Sara stopped looking at her phone and stared at her husband. The look of concern on her face made Victor want to take back his words.

"The last three people who have died from our class all have two things in common. Ruby came to see them before they died, and they were all friends of mine."

Sara rolled her eyes, but Victor saw a glimmer behind her expression. Deep down, she knew something wasn't right. The last person Ruby had visited was Scott. He'd been holed up at his house with a broken leg.

"Victor, we are getting to the age where people that we knew in school are going to die. It is inevitable." Sara said. She turned from him and looked back at her phone.

"Ya, I get it. But the people that have died were perfectly healthy before she saw them. You don't think it's weird that the only thing that was wrong with Scott was a broken leg. Then she shows up, and he's dead in a month? Not to mention, what about Mary and Chuck. Both healthy people who got sick. Not deadly sick, just the flu in both cases. She shows up…" Victor traced his index finger over his throat. Scott barely talked to me the last week of his life. Don't you think that's weird? We spoke every day.

Sara moved in closer to Victor and put her arm around him and hugged tight. "Honey, I know you are grieving for your friends. Scott was the best, but this line of thinking isn't healthy, and it is not going to bring him back. Mary, Chuck, and Scott were not depressed people. They wouldn't have wanted you to go on like this." Now it was Victor's turn to roll his eyes. Sara hit his shoulder again and sighed.

"Babe, she's a grief counselor. She was just doing her job and trying to be there for a friend." Sara let go of his shoulder and got up from the couch. "I'm going to bed."

"Do you think that Scott needed a grief counselor for his broken leg? Or the other two for the flu? Scott was a bonehead who broke his leg snowboarding because he was too high to get down the slope in one piece. He didn't need a grief counselor."

"She was his friend," Sara said.

"He hadn't been her friend for a very long time."

Sara kissed Scott on the forehead. "Come up to bed soon."

Victor watched as his wife walked out of the room. Her head down, looking at her phone as she did. Victor always liked to watch her do this. He couldn't believe she never walked into the wall. Victor wanted to follow her, and he wished he were tired, but he didn't see that happening anytime soon.

"Dead from a broken leg." Victor blew air out through his teeth. He knew damn well that wasn't what happened. He just needed to prove it. Victor turned off the end table light and sat back on the couch. His eyes were closed in the dark, but his mind was wide open.

****

Get them all, and you will be whole!

Ruby Worklow's eyes always snapped open at precisely 6:00 a.m. on the dot. They had for over twenty years, and the catalyst was usually a dream like the one that was fading into the ether of her brain right now as she threw the threadbare ratty thing, she called a blanket off of her large frame. She swung her big feet to the cold hardwood floor and relished in the sensation. Anything she could feel was a good experience. For two decades, she'd been as numb and hallow as a store mannequin. Acting a part that she knew people wanted or needed to see. She could pretend to care, and she could fake being normal. But other than the cold, numb feeling, the only other emotion that Ruby felt was sadness. She put on a smile and kept going out into the world.

She shuffled over to her small bathroom without hardly a sound. She was big, but she possessed the nimbleness of a house cat. No one ever heard Ruby coming. You would be talking to a friend on a street corner one day thinking you were the only two people in the world, and in an instant, you would jump, and your words would catch in your throat as you looked up at the large smiling woman staring at you. Ruby could sneak, and she loved to do it.

She bent down and looked at the vanity mirror in her bathroom. She contemplated her face. She was getting older, but there wasn't a line on her porcelain-like skin. Her mother, who had been of average size, had always said that Ruby had skin that most women would have killed for in an instant. Ruby would smile and then frown almost instantly when the woman would follow it up with, at least you got that going for you, my dear. Ruby was glad her mother was gone.

She rubbed her face and looked away from the mirror. No going down memory lane today, Ruby, she thought. You have a lot of people to help today. A lot of people need your help. Ruby took off the large nightgown that was just as threadbare as her blanket and let it fall to the floor in a large pile and got into the shower. She didn't wait for the water to get hot. The cold water felt good on her skin. Ruby let her mind wander. She thought about all the people that she had helped, and she grinned. The cold water splashed against her face and teeth.

****

Victor took the day off from work and didn't tell Sara. He didn't want his wife to know what he was going to do. She would have questioned his sanity if she knew he would follow Ruby Worklow all day like some horrible amateur detective.

He'd gotten Ruby's address from the latest High School reunion website. Information like this was easy to get in this day and age. A couple of keywords and you were officially a stalker. Victor felt like one as he waited outside of Ruby's apartment building. He'd been waiting since the sun came up. Sara hadn't thought anything of him getting up early because sometimes Victor had to go into the shop first when a job needed to get finished. His wife had groaned and rolled over when he'd kissed her on the cheek to say goodbye. She hadn't said word one.

At just passed six-thirty, the door of the apartment building opened, and Ruby in all her six foot five glory stepped through the doorway. Victor took in an intake of breath. Had she gotten bigger, he asked himself. Every time he saw the woman, he gazed in amazement. Ruby was larger than life. That was the reason she was so good at her job, Victor thought. The woman hypnotized you with her sheer size. Victor thought he recalled when Ruby had been smaller, but no images wanted to come to the surface of his mind. He thought he'd remembered someone saying she had a glandular problem, but he couldn't be sure.

Victor watched as she took long strides down the street. He assumed this was her usual way to work. He followed, trying to keep an eye on Ruby and still stay out of her line of sight. She was easy to follow. Ruby's head stuck up over the cars parked on the side of the street. The people that walked around her were dwarfed as they passed on the sidewalk. Victor watched as people stared up at the giantess. Their eyes wide and mouths open in dumb expressions. One woman almost walked into a parked car as she looked back over her shoulder, mesmerized by Ruby. Her hip nudged the bumper of a Toyota, and the lady made a harumph sound. After rubbing the side of her leg, she turned back around. Her head was looking left and right to see if anyone had seen her banging into the car. Victor giggled as he passed the lady. The woman scowled at him, but it only made Victor laugh harder.

He lost sight of Ruby for a moment, and a shock of panic bloomed in his chest. He looked up just in time to see Ruby walk into one of the coffee houses that seemed to reside on every corner of the street. This one was called "Grind My Gears." Victor rolled his eyes and went to stand behind one of the cars parked on the curb. The wind was cold. He pushed the collar of his jacket up and tried to push his body deeper into his coat. The logical part of his mind tried to be a voice of reason as he stood there. What are you hoping to find out? Why don't you just go to the police? Every valid question that popped into his head, Victor shot down or just outright ignored. He knew deep down that his friends didn't die naturally, and Ruby was somehow connected. It was too much of a coincidence that they had all been friends with Ruby at one point in time. If he went to the police, they might listen to him, but they weren't going to do anything. He was on his own.

After five minutes, Victor's ears felt like they were going to fall off, and he contemplated leaving. He rubbed them, feeling hot pins and needles as he did. He cursed himself for not bringing a hat. He was just about to say to heck with it when Ruby came out of the coffee house. Victor looked at the steam coming off of her cup and felt a pang of envy. He wanted to get himself a cup, but the big lady was already halfway down the block. Coffee would have to wait.

Victor followed Ruby for two blocks before she turned into a large parking lot. At the end of the parking lot sat what looked like a big office building. Victor saw the sign on the top of the roof. It said Caldwell Arms Apartments. It was one of those buildings that the super hip (or people that thought of themselves that way) lived in so they could be within walking distances of hip hot spots. A converted commercial building turned into snooty apartments. Victor watched from the entrance of the parking lot as Ruby took long strides and was at the front of the building in no time. She rang the buzzer, waited a moment, and then the door buzzed again, and Ruby entered the building.

Victor ran across the parking lot to the front of the building. He peered through the glass on the building's door. He could make out Ruby's massive shoes as they climbed the steps inside the building's lobby. Victor paused and looked at the building's doorbell panel. He hadn't thought any of this through, and he had no idea what to do at the moment. Victor contemplated hitting all the buttons. He saw it in a movie once where a guy hit all the buzzers, and somebody not paying attention had buzzed the guy into the building. It seemed easy enough, Victor thought. He was just about to try it when the door opened. Victor looked at the person in the open door, and then he looked up.

"Victor?" Ruby's smiling but confused face stared down at him. "What are you doing here?"

Victor's throat felt thick, and he could feel his face getting flushed. He had to think fast, he thought. "Oh, Ruby. How have you been?"

Ruby tilted her head to the side. Victor had a dog who used to do the same thing when it was thinking. "I'm great. What are you doing here?"

"Ah, had an estimate to do for, you know what, I forgot the guy's name." Victor turned his head and looked at the panel of apartments. He picked the first name he saw. "Jensen." He saw that the name had an H in front of it. "Ya, Harold Jensen."

"Hmm, I know a Haley Jensen that lives here."

"Yup, that's the one," Victor said. His delivery was a little too quick. He thought if Ruby believed this, she wasn't what he thought, couldn't be a killer if you were that dumb.

She smiled at him and reached out and patted his shoulder. Victor was glad he hadn't flinched; it took everything in him to not. "Well, glad I could help. It was good seeing you. I wish I could talk more, but I got to get to work. Tell Sara, I said hello." The sun was blotted out from the sky for a moment as Ruby walked past Victor on the stairs.

"See ya," Victor said to the woman's back. Ruby turned slightly, still walking, and looked at Victor with the biggest smile on her face and winked. A cold chill, that was amazingly colder than the weather went down his spine. Her head turned quickly, and she was out of the parking lot and around the corner before Victor could get his bearings. He sat down on the steps of the apartment. All the energy Victor had was taken out of him. He felt sick to his stomach and decided he wasn't going to go to work. He'd tell Sara he didn't feel well, which wasn't a lie. Victor trudged the mile and a half back to his car and cursed himself the whole way for not being better at concealing himself.

****

Victor had never stayed home from the shop for this long, Sara thought. He'd skipped a couple of days here and there but never a full-on week. Sara figured he wasn't going to go in today either, judging by the dark circles his eye sockets had become. She'd heard him last night in the living room. He'd been mumbling to himself when she came down to ask if he was coming to bed soon. He'd mumbled something else, and then Sara had gone back upstairs. She hadn't said much to him about not going to work because he was the owner of the place, but he'd told her numerous times that when he wasn't there, the place fell apart. House painters don't make good project managers, Sara, he'd told her once. Enough was enough.

"Victor." Her husband kept staring out the window. A butter knife and a piece of burnt toast were in his hands. "Victor."

"Huh." Victor turned towards her, a confused faraway look on his face.

"What's going on, hun? You haven't been to the shop in over a week. You're not sleeping… You're really starting to scare me, Babe."

Victor's look of confusion turned into annoyance. "I'm taking some time. Greg has control of the shop. You don't think I check-in, but I do."

Greg was Victor's younger brother; it made Sara feel a little bit better knowing he was running things. "Well, that's good. But what about you? Babe, you don't look good. I think you should go to the doctor."

"Oh, give me a break," Victor said. He threw the piece of toast and the butter knife into the sink. The clatter of the silverware hurt Sara's ears and fired up her anger at the same time.

"You give me a break. You have been acting weird, and you look like shit, Victor, ever since you came home from work earlier last week. What the hell happened?"

"Sara…" Victor's throat made a clicking noise as his words stopped midway up his throat.

Sara shook her head. "I got to get to work. I'll call you later. Victor, if you don't snap out of this, I'll have your brother drag you to the doctor." Sara grabbed her purse and walked out the front door of the house. It took a walk to the car and the drive to her office to make her feel like not crying.

"Hey, Sara."

Sara looked up just in time to see Marcy before running into her. The poor lady banged her knee on one of the desks as she tried to get out of Sara's way. A regular occurrence for Sara's friend. The woman was always banging into something.

"Are you okay, Mar," Sara said.

Her friend rubbed the side of her leg and then looked up, her grimace turning into one of concern. "I should be asking you that. Have you been crying?"

Sara wiped both her eyes self-consciously. "Ya, just dumb stuff with Victor."

"Do you need me to kick him a little," Marcy said. Sara knew she was joking, but her friend had a look of determination on her face that made her smile.

"No. You'd end up kicking yourself somehow." Sara and Marcy shared a silent moment, then they both busted up laughing. Marcy mimicked herself, trying to kick someone and pretended to kick the desk she'd bumped her shin on, which made Sara laugh harder. Marcy could always make her laugh. She was almost like the funny little sister that Sara never had. She was a fun friend, and she kept Sara feeling young. Sara stopped laughing for a moment and grabbed the side of the reception desk.

"Ah, man, Mar, you kill me," Sara said.

"Not my intention, boss," Marcy said.

"What have I told you about calling me that. It makes me sound like a jerk." Sara said.

"I know, just giving you some crap. I had to bring us back up from the depths of desperate laughter."

Sara patted the young lady on the shoulder, walking past her to her office next to the reception desk where Sara resided. She opened her office door and threw her purse on her messy desk that seemed to contain every building inspection in the city and walked to the back of the building to the small kitchenette.

"I already made coffee," Marcy shouted from the front of the office.

"That's my girl," Sara shouted back.

Sara was pouring her first cup of coffee for the day when she heard the front door security bell chime making her spill some of her coffee on the counter. Sara quickly wiped it up as she listened to the murmured voices of Marcy and the early morning visitor. Sara sighed as she threw the coffee-stained napkin into the wastebasket by the door. "Guess I don't even get to drink my coffee in peace today," She said.

Sara walked back to the front of the building and almost dropped all of her coffee a second time when she saw who stood blocking out most of the light from the office's front windows.

"Ruby," Sara said almost under her breath.

Ruby smiled. "Sara, it's been so long. It's terrific to see you."

Sara had never really liked Ruby in school or otherwise. There had always been something wrong with her, Sara thought. She wasn't as paranoid as Victor, but something was just below the surface with this one. "Can I help you." Sara blurted out.

"Maybe you could help me. Can we talk in your office?" Sara looked at Marcy, who looked back at her with an uncomfortable smile on her face, a reaction that most people gave Ruby when they first met her.

Sara looked back at Ruby. "Sure, Marcy, can you handle the front while I talk to Ruby."

Marcy nodded her head. "Sure, no sweat." Her eyes got huge and she turned back around, not looking at Ruby.

Sara motioned for Ruby to come around the desk and into her office. Sara sat her coffee down, and then sat looking at the door. Ruby's large frame entered the doorway, and the woman had to bend down to get through. Sara tried to conceal her astonishment as she watched. She motioned in front of her to one of the chairs that sat in front of her desk. Ruby smiled and sat instantly, making the chair she sat in look like it for kindergarteners. Sara heard the chair groan and said a silent prayer for it not to break.

"So, Ruby, what can I do for you," Sara said.

"I saw Victor last week. He was following me." Ruby said. She'd lost her smile, and she stared hard at Sara.

Sara felt the blood run out of her head, and she felt instantly dizzy. So, this was the reason for the weird behavior. Sara felt an odd betrayal even though she knew that him following Ruby wasn't to have an affair. She felt betrayed because he hadn't come to her and been honest about what he'd been doing.

"Where did you see him?" Sara asked. She tried to keep her voice from shaking, but she wasn't doing a good job about it.

"It was out in front of one of my friend's apartment building, but I'd saw him tailing me the whole time," Ruby said.

Sara had gotten over the initial shock of hearing her husband had gone amateur detective and was now getting annoyed. "What is it that you want me to do, Ruby?"

"I'd like to help Sara. I think Victor needs to talk to someone. I got the feeling he was working through some things."

Sara was taken aback by Ruby's blunt and intuitive reply. She was just about to tell her to get the hell out of her office, but Ruby held up her hand.

"I'm sorry if I've offended you. I just want to help. I have a feeling with Victor, something that I have seen before." Ruby turned away from Sara's gaze.

I can't argue with the woman, Sara thought. There is something very wrong with Victor, and the woman sitting before her would know how to spot a person that needed help. The woman is a trained therapist.

Ruby looked back at Sara and then looked down at her purse. She rummaged through it for a few seconds and pulled out a gleaming white business card. In a quick, graceful motion, she handed the card to Sara. The card was pretty basic. It had Ruby's name, email, and phone perfectly centered on the card. Under that were the words, I just want to help, written in gold. Sara couldn't help but smile as she looked at the gold letters

"If you need anything, don't hesitate to call me. Or if you just feel like talking." Ruby said.

Sara felt warm tears starting to form at the edges of her eyes. "He hasn't gone to work in almost two weeks, and he hasn't been sleeping." The word fell out of her mouth. She couldn't believe she was telling Ruby any of this. It felt like the woman's voice had plucked the words out of her throat.

Ruby sighed and nodded her head. "This is pretty normal, considering Victor has been grieving for three people. That could throw anyone into a deep depression."

"Victor…" Sara stopped herself. Ruby sat forward, and Sara felt herself wanting to tell her everything like Ruby was a six-foot-five Barbara Walters. Once again, the words were drawn out of her. "He thinks you have something to do with their deaths." Sara laughed nervously and sat back in her chair.

Ruby's eyes looked sad, and Sara instantly felt terrible about what she had confessed.

"I can see why he thinks that." Ruby said.

Sara couldn't stop her eyebrows from raising. A touch of ice ran up her back. "What…?"

"Well, while I talked to our mutual friends, I assure you all I did was talk to each one of them."

Sara felt better than just moments before when she thought this big woman would confess to three murders. She let out a long breath she'd been holding and ran her hand through her hair. She watched as Ruby looked out the window.

"I tried to help them." Ruby's lip quivered, and Sara felt sudden anger toward Victor. She reached out and grabbed the tissues she kept on the side of the desk and offered them to Ruby. She grabbed one in her hand, making the tissue look almost miniature.

The woman dabbed her eyes. "I think I could help Victor. I'd like to talk to both you guys if you'd have me."

Sara felt any trepidation she'd had with this woman slowly melt away. She couldn't think of a better thing to do than have Victor talk to Ruby. Then he would see that she was just a regular woman who just wanted to help people. She was grieving, just like Victor.

"I think that is a great idea. How does tonight sound?" Sara couldn't help but smile when she saw the surprise in Ruby's face.

"Well, I think that sounds great."

After Ruby left, Sara contemplated calling Victor and chewing him out, but she decided to wait. She didn't want him to try to get out of seeing Ruby tonight. Sara looked up when she heard a knock on her door frame.

Marcy was standing there with her hand on her stomach. Her face was pale and almost had a greenish tint to it. Her friend looked like she had aged five years in the last thirty minutes.

"I'm not feeling so hot," Marcy said.

"You don't look so hot, Mar." Sara did a quick inventory in her head. There wasn't much she couldn't handle by herself today. "Why don't you go home and get some rest. I'll give you a call later to see how you're doing." Marcy didn't talk. She only nodded her head. Sara listened as she grabbed her things off her desk and then went out the front door.

"Geez, I hope it isn't catchy." She said to the empty room.

****

Victor's thoughts had been dark ever since he'd seen Ruby last Monday. Snatches of scenes played out in his head of visions of winged creatures with large sharp teeth and thirsty mouths. He hadn't slept for a day and a half because his dreams were even worse. What had she done to him, he thought? All he could muster lately was sitting on the couch and staring out the window.

The mummified remains of Haley Jensen were found in her apartment this morning. The police say the woman had been seen by neighbors the week before and are baffled by the condition of her remains. We will follow up on this case as information comes in, now here's Bill with the weather…

"That's where I saw her! She killed that woman!" Victor said. His head swooned as icy bands of chills went up his back and deposited themselves at the base of his skull. He was almost bouncing on the couch. He hadn't exuded that much energy in over a week.

This has to stop, he thought. An idea popped into his head. He knew where she lived. He could go there and simply let himself into her apartment. Victor wouldn't let himself say break-in. He was doing this for the greater good. Victor dropped his robe on the living room floor and went upstairs to take a shower and change. Ruby had to be brought to justice. Nothing was left of his rational voice inside of his head. The voice that told you the things that you were planning were an unbelievably bad idea. Victor had moved into crazy town and become a permanent resident.

****

Victor parked his car directly in front of Ruby's building, no longer caring if the woman saw him. He pushed up his collar against the cold wind and stared up into the windows of the building and walked across the street with his head down. He was feeling more and more like a common criminal with each stride. He knew Ruby wasn't home, but he didn't want any noisy neighbors asking him questions. He was going to get into her apartment, have a look around, and get the hell out. Victor put his hand around the lock picking kit his brother had given him a few Christmases ago. He'd laughed at the gag gift when he'd opened the box, but now he was glad to have it.

He stared at the buzzer board and ran his finger down the panel until he saw R. Worklow. He'd forgotten Ruby's name, and a smirk went across his face. In high school, he'd always thought it was an odd name. Even weirder that he'd forgotten it. Weirder still was that Victor couldn't remember Ruby even being around the years before his junior year of high school. He was sure beyond a shadow of a doubt that he'd gone to elementary school with her. All those years seemed to be missing from his memory. He was missing a whole piece of time, and it nagged at his soul.

Victor pressed the buzzer and waited a minute just to be sure that she wasn't home. He turned back towards the street and tried to act casual. A trickle of sweat ran down his back. The contrast of the cool fabric of his shirt and hot sweat made him shiver.

This is crazy, he thought. I need to go home. He jumped when he heard the door of the building open. Victor turned around and saw a lady with a stroller, struggling with the door. Victor ran over and grabbed the door just before it banged into the stroller.

"Here, let me help you with that," Victor said. He grabbed the front of the cart and guided it while the lady pushed the remainder through the doors opening.

"Oh, thank you." The young mother said in a hushed voice. "I just got her to sleep."

Victor smiled his best boy scout smile, all the while, feeling like some monster lurking on the apartment stairs. "No problem whatsoever. Have a good day." Victor said.

The woman looked at him and smiled. She pushed the stroller in front of her. She never looked back.

Victor let himself into the lobby and scanned the small rectangular mailboxes, looking again for Ruby's name. The last one, on the end, said plainly Worklow and had the number 32 in gold numerals plastered on the front. Victor looked around the small room. The space only contained the mailboxes and a flight of dull-looking stairs that faced directly in front of him. The building only had three floors, so he figured that Ruby's apartment was probably on the floor directly above him. He took a deep breath and started to walk up the stairs.

Ruby's apartment was down the first hallway. Victor walked slowly and tried to look like he belonged in the building. He made it to Ruby's door without being interrupted.

Victor stood in front of the brown door with a big 32 right above the peephole. Weird anxiety came over him as he stared at the small hole. He imagined that Ruby was looking at him from the other side, making him take big breaths of air. He put his hand against the door to steady himself and almost started hyperventilating when the door pushed into the apartment beyond. Victor felt chills go up his back and sweat instantly broke out on his forehead as he stood watching the apartment door squeak open, revealing a small kitchen to the right and a front room directly ahead. A cold puff of air pushed its way out through the threshold of the door. The apartment was freezing. It was colder than the outside.

Victor walked in the door and cupped his hands over his mouth and blew warm air into them. He didn't want to mess with his gloves in case he had to pick something up. He was looking for anything. Evidence that could link Ruby to the deaths of the four people. Victor walked further in and saw that the apartment had a single room off to the left of the front room. The door to the room was closed and looked even more ominous than the front door of the apartment.

"You came here to see Victor. Well, now, we shall see." He said to the cold room.

Victor walked over and put his hand on the knob of the door and immediately pulled it back. If his hand had been wet, it would have stuck to the doorknob. He reached into his jacket pocket and brought out one of his gloves and put it on. He reached for the door again and turned the knob. He had to use all the strength in his hand just to get it to turn a little bit of the way. He pushed on the door, and it didn't budge. He would have to try it with his body, he thought. Victor reared back and put his shoulder into the flimsy door. The wood gave way with a crack, and Victor almost fell headfirst into a large dresser.

The room was freezing and had a slight rotten fruit smell, which Victor thought was odd because nothing could rot in here. This room was like a walk-in freezer. He scanned the small bedroom. The layout was the same as any other bedroom where the large bed took up most of the room. It was the room of a person without much of a personality.

Victor was about to abandon his plan and leave when he looked back to the dresser. Carved in the wood was something he hadn't seen in years, since his junior year of high school. It was an Ouija board, he thought. Just like… Victor touched the wood of the dresser, and Ruby's bedroom dissolved around him. He couldn't fight the pull.

"Victor. Earth to Victor. Hello Victor."

Victor stared out of eyes that weren't his own. Or they hadn't been for a long time. His best friend Scott sat across. A younger Scott with hair and not a strand of facial hair. He remembered this scene in his life almost immediately. He was sixteen. They were in the abandoned house down the street that everyone thought was haunted, and Ruby… He watched as the eyes looked to their right. Ruby Worklow sat next to him. She was wearing a sundress that looked big on her petite body. She smiled at him, and Victor remembered how it had made him feel when Ruby smiled at him. A flood of memories that had been lurking below the surface for years came flooding back. Ruby in elementary school. Victor and her being next-door neighbors. Victor saw Ruby as something else in junior high school. Then he remembered hurried breath and sweaty make-out sessions in high school. He remembered her hair smelled like strawberry shampoo and that she was strong when her father had died.

Victor felt the loss. How could he have forgotten? How could they all have forgotten? He thought. Oh, Ruby. I'm so sorry. The girl in front of him was a miniature version of the Ruby Victor had come to know later in life.

Young Ruby smiled a warm smile that would have made young Victor stupid for a second. "Are you going to play, Victor?"

"Victor won't play. He's a big wuss."

The eyes turned to the voice source, and Victor saw young versions of Mary and Chuck. They were sitting close together. Victor couldn't remember them ever being apart.

The Victor that was now, felt his younger self's lips move and heard his young, just done with voice. "Shut up, Mary. I was the one who had the idea." The eyes looked down, and Victor saw the Ouija board. Old Victor knew what would happen, and he wanted to stop it, but this had already happened. There was no stopping it now. He tried to yell out to tell them to stop, but he was not in control. The planchette sat in the middle of the board, and impending doom washed over him.

"We all have to put our hands on it. Otherwise, it won't work." Mary said.

The eyes scanned his friends' faces. As if on cue, everyone leaned forward and put their hands on the plastic guide.

"Do we ask a question?" Ruby said.

The planchette started to move by itself. Slowly at first, but then it picked up speed. Old Victor could hear his young friends and his young self, reciting the letters as the game piece rolled over them.

I-A-M-H-E-R-E

"Scott, you are such a dork. I know you're moving it."

"No, I'm not." Scott's voice sounded dry. The eyes looked up. Scott's face had turned white as a sheet.

"Guys, this is scaring me," Ruby said.

The eyes turned toward Ruby. Victor could feel the slight pull of a smile on young Victor's face. "It's okay." He heard his younger self say.

The eyes turned back to board. "What is your name." Young Victor said.

Once again, everyone recited the letters.

Y-O-U-K-N-O-W-W-H-O-I-A-M

"Guys, I want to stop," Ruby said. The planchette went into a frenzy, moving almost quicker than they could keep up.

I-A-M-H-E-R-E-F-O-R-R-U-B-Y

Ruby gasped and tried to pull her hands away from the planchette; everyone's hands came away but hers. Her scream turned into a low growl that seemed to originate from her stomach. Her face contorted into a horrific caricature of what had once been her face. White foam jetted out of her mouth while her entire body shook violently. Victor watched as his young self wrestled her hands-free from the planchette. He remembered that he thought this would stop whatever was happening to Ruby, but her body still shook.

She fell to the floor. Victor remembered he thought she looked like a fish he'd caught once. It had flopped so hard it flew out of his father's boat and back into the water. Ruby bore a striking resemblance.

"She's having a seizure," Mary said.

Victor reached out and tried to steady Ruby, but she had grown so strong that he couldn't keep her down. The girl's mouth snapped out and clamped onto his hand. He barely had time to react. He felt two large fangs sink deep into his palm. Victor looked down at the gargoyle that had taken up residence in his girlfriend. Her eyes were red and wide. Victor screamed out, and the Ruby thing let go of his hand and fell back onto the floor.

"I can smell all your souls." The Ruby thing said. The voice was one of an ancient old witch.

That was when they had run—and forgotten. Like a magic trick, the Ruby they had known had ceased to exist.

Victor felt a sucking sensation, and he woke up next to his car, sitting on the curb. His whole body was stiff, and his ass was numb from the concrete. A long line of drool ran from his lip to the street. He wiped absentmindedly with the back of his hand.

He remembered. He didn't know why he'd forgotten, but he remembered.

They had all ran out of the old house, and as soon as they'd gotten to the street, that was it, Victor thought. He'd woken up the next morning with no recollection of the incident. He hadn't even remembered his teenage love, Ruby.

Victor got slowly to his feet and wiped a tear from his eye. Something had gotten into her that night, and they had run away. Ran away when she needed them most, Victor thought. He had to make it right. He fished into his pocket for car keys, needing to get home. He and Sara were in danger.

****

Not one of the house lights were on when Sara pulled into the driveway. Victor's car was not in its spot either. She didn't want to deal with where he went and what he did, so she opened her car door and put it out of her mind. He would be along soon, and they could have their argument and be done with it, hopefully before Ruby came over.

Sara walked to the front door and fished her keys out of her purse. She put her key in the slot, and something in her, some deep and ancient instinct told her to pull the key out and run to the car. Sara paused and took a deep breath. Victor's paranoia is rubbing off on me, she thought.

She opened the door and flipped on the outside light and the front room light. She took her shoes off and closed the door. The deadbolt locked itself, and Sara jumped back from it and screamed.

"Come sit, Sara."

The voice made Sara scream again, and she whirled around and pushed her back to the front door. She clutched her purse to her face and stared over it.

Ruby was in the middle of the room. A game board laid at her feet. When Sara looked closer, she realized it was a Ouija board.

"Why are you in my house?" Sara said. Her voice shook on each word.

"You invited me, Sara. Don't you remember?" Ruby said.

The woman standing before her seemed bigger than the one she talked to at her office just a few hours before. Her face was different, as well. The lines of her jaw and brow were no longer soft and feminine. They had taken on simian traits. Ruby looked demonic.

"I did, but I didn't think you'd break into my house," Sara said.

The laugh that came out of Ruby was guttural, and it made Sara want to break the door down and run away screaming.

"Victor will be along in a minute and then we'll play." Ruby's big smile exposed long pointed teeth.

Sara tried to push even further into the front door. Her hand flew up and fumbled with the lock. Ruby was beside her with such speed that Sara never even saw her move. She was on the other side of the room one minute and then standing next to her.

Ruby put her clawed hand against Sara's cheek. Sara whimpered as the thing's sharp-bladed nails rain down the soft part of her neck. "I'm not here for you. But if you don't sit down, my dear, I will snap your neck like a brittle branch in fall." The thing's voice was morphing from Ruby's to something disgusting. Something from the depths of the underworld. The woman's breath smelled of sulfur, and her clothes looked burnt. Sara knew then that Ruby wasn't in control anymore.

Sara let herself be moved by the disgusting thing. It sat her on the couch parallel with the Ouija board. She hitched in-breaths and tried to calm herself.

"You don't get to play, my dear. You are here to witness my revenge."

The Ruby thing smiled down at her, and Sara felt the first bit of her sanity drain away like water in an undertow.

****

Victor's hands shook on the steering wheel as he pulled next to Sara's car. The whole ride over had been taken up with snatches of memories that he hadn't thought of for more than twenty years. He didn't know why they had all forgotten Ruby, but he remembered now. She had a right to her vengeance, Victor thought.

He had barely put his truck in park before he was opening the door. He threw the gear shift into park, making the tires squeak on the concrete and throwing him against the open door. The bang against the door brought him back up to this reality. Get a grip, Victor. If you don't calm down, you're going to end up running yourself over, he thought.

Victor ran to the front door. As soon as he put his hand on the doorknob, it pulled out of his hand. The door swung open fast, and he stood staring at a red blouse. Victor slowly looked up and saw the distorted face of Ruby. The same face he'd seen that night so long ago. She smiled, and Victor saw that the Ruby thing had pointed teeth. Not just fangs, every one of her teeth was needle-sharp. A hand clamped onto his shoulder, and Victor was lifted off the ground and thrown through the door before he could cry out. He heard the door slam behind him as he fell to the ground.

"Long time no see Victor. Ready to play a game?" The Ruby thing said. The words sounded odd, like a half growl and half pleasant voice that had hypnotized so many people.

Victor looked to the left and saw that Sara was tied up and gagged on the sofa. Her eyes streamed tears, and Victor wanted to go to her and hold her. Tell her everything was going to be okay. He knew that if he moved this thing that had once been Ruby would be on him in a second. He pushed himself up slowly and sat on the floor with his back against the end table of the couch.

"What happened to you?" Victor said.

"I think you know what happened to me. I realize you four conveniently forgot about that night. I would have thought the dresser in my room would have jogged your memory.

"I remember. And I'm so sorry. We were scared kids." Victor said. His voice came out in a pleading manner that he wasn't embarrassed by, something in him said it was a good thing if this Ruby thing knew he was scared.

"So was I!" The thing screamed, and Victor pressed further against the end table. Sara made a whimpering sound on the other end of the couch. "So was I, Victor, when you three left me there on that dirty floor." Ruby's demonic face was right in front of his now. Her eyes had gone red. "What you see before you isn't totally me. The real me exists in a dark place. The real me is scared and confused. What you see is the shell of me. The thing that came out of that board is in me. It has been for a very long time. The only way it will leave me and give me that other piece is if I get all the other players into that dark place."

Victor scooted back further. He could see the veins popping out of the Ruby thing's forehead. "Ruby, we can fix this together. We can do this together."

An ear-shattering scream that turned into a laugh came out of Ruby's mouth. Victor pressed his hands over his ears, and he heard Sara cry out in pain.

"You didn't care for twenty years. It is time for you to feel the pain, the numbness…"

Victor was going to plead some more, but he was distracted by the planchette on the board. It was spinning faster and faster on the board. As it turned, it started to glow a bright purple light that was pleasant at first but then started to hurt Victor's eyes.

"Put your hands on it, Victor." The Ruby thing said. Its face was even more grotesque in the purple glow.

"No, please."

The thing's clawed hand shot out and grabbed Victor's wrist and yanked his arm onto the game piece, Victor tried to pull his hand away, but it stuck to the piece. He screamed out as the thing that was Ruby grabbed his other hand and placed it to on the piece. Now both of his hands were stuck to the piece. The purple light got brighter, and Victor saw his fingers disappear inside of the planchette. He screamed and started to squirm and pull like a bear stuck in a trap. Victor heard Sara's muffled scream and looked up. In the purple hue of the room, he saw his three other dead friends. Their faces were all drawn and purple—the faces of mummies.

"This is what it felt like, Victor." The Ruby thing screamed as Victor was sucked into the game piece up to his forearms.

"No! Please, ruby, I'm sorry."

"The monster, the dark lord, wants what he wants, Victor." The smile on Ruby's face was crazed, and Victor knew there was no saving him now. Wherever this portal went to would be where he dwelled. He would be punished for his sins.

As soon as the planchette got to Victor's elbow, it went fast. Sara watched as the last bit of Victor went down into the Ouija board planchette, and the last bit of her sanity went down the drain.

****

The woman rolled out into the sun on a fine spring day in April at the Satori Hills Mental Health Facility would not have been recognized by her friend and former secretary, if a nice young man at the reception desk hadn't told her who she was.

Marcy walked slowly to the wheelchair that sat in the middle of a pretty garden lush with flowers. Marcy thought about how nice it must be to get to sit here all day and just relax. Then she saw her friend.

Sara looked twenty years older. Her body formed the shape of the chair she sat in, day in and day out. Her facial muscles drooped, and dark circles had taken up permanent residence under her eyes. Marcy always wanted to run when she came to see Sara. Every time she came to see Sara, her friend's appearance had gotten worse. But she did what she thought Sara would have done for her, and she came and talked about the goings-on and inform her friend about the office that was now closed.

"How ya doing today, sweety?" Marcy said. She pushed a bit of Sara's hair back and around her ear. She used a bib that was strapped around her friends' neck to wipe away some spit accumulated on her lip.

"I know I came by just a few days ago, but I wanted to let you know I found a job. You'll never guess who I'll be working for." Marcy waited for her friend to reply with an answer, fully knowing that there wouldn't be one. "I got a call yesterday from that lady that came in just before…" Marcy trailed off, not wanting to recount the home break-in that had landed her friend here and Victor God knows where. He'd simply vanished as if in thin air. "Anyway, I got a call from Ruby."

A single tear rolled down Sara's face. Marcy wiped it absentmindedly and told her friend all about her new job.

2 ABOUT THE AUTHOR

Ernie Howard was born on January 29,1977, during a Minnesota blizzard. His two story telling parents almost didn't make it to the hospital in their beat-up blue Cadillac. Ernie is the author of The Pool, A World Without, Walter, Float, On Holiday with an S.O.B. The Night Portals series, as well as other titles. All of these books are available on Kindle. Ernie lives with his wife and 3 boys in Henderson, NV, where he dreams up new stories and tries to live every day to the fullest.

Have any questions? Want to say hello? Connect with me below.

Facebook:
https://facebook.com/ErnieWritesBooks/

Website:
https://erniehowardwrites.com